Alexander Pushkin

PAINTINGS BY Gennady Spirin

First published in the United States 1996 by Dial Books
A Division of Penguin Books USA Inc.
375 Hudson Street / New York, New York 10014

Published in Germany 1995 by Verlag J. F. Schreiber as
Das Märchen vom Zaren Saltan
Copyright © 1995 by Verlag J. F. Schreiber
American text copyright © 1996 by Dial Books
Based on a translation by Pauline Hejl / All rights reserved
Typography by Amelia Lau Carling
Printed in Belgium / First Edition
1 3 5 7 9 10 8 6 4 2

Library of Congress Cataloging in Publication Data
Pushkin, Aleksandr Sergeevich, 1799–1837.
[Skazka o tsare Saltane. English]
The tale of Tsar Saltan / by Alexander Pushkin; paintings by Gennady Spirin.
—1st ed. p. cm.
"Based on a translation by Pauline Hejl"—T. p. verso.
Summary: Betrayed by her jealous sisters, a tsarina and her
infant son are marooned on a barren island until a magical
swan helps them regain their rightful heritage.
ISBN 0-8037-2001-7 (trade: alk.paper)
[1. Fairy tales. 2. Folklore—Russia.] I. Spirin, Gennadii, ill. II. Title.
PZ8.P976Taj 1996   398.2'0947'02—dc20   [E]   95-38661   CIP   AC

The art for this book was prepared with watercolors.

The Tale of
TSAR SALTAN

DIAL BOOKS · NEW YORK

Once upon a time there were three sisters who sat near a window at their looms and talked of their dreams.

"If I were the tsar's wife, I would have a magnificent feast and invite everyone!" said one of the sisters.

"And if I became the tsarina, I would spin the finest linen for everyone," said the second sister.

Then the youngest girl said, "Oh, if I became the tsarina, I would wish to have a son who was strong and brave."

Suddenly the door opened and Tsar Saltan entered the room. He had heard the three girls talking, and the words of the youngest sister had touched him deeply.

"You will be my wife!" he exclaimed. "But I will not take you away from your sisters. One of them can be a cook and the other a weaver at my court."

That annoyed the two older sisters very much, but hiding their feelings, they followed the tsar and their younger sister to the tsar's court.

The wedding took place soon after they arrived,
and many guests celebrated with the tsar and his bride.

Before long the youngest sister's wish was granted,
and she knew that she would give birth to the tsar's child.

Then, however, a war broke out and the tsar had to
leave his young wife. Begging her to take good care of
herself, he mounted his horse and rode off with his men.

The tsar was away for a long time, and the tsarina's
sisters had plenty of time to nurse their grudges. Together
with the tsar's cousin, who was also a jealous woman,
they made terrible plans to destroy the tsarina.

Time passed, and the tsarina gave birth to a son—
a big, strong boy. Full of joy, she sent a message to her
husband. But the cook and the weaver intercepted it,
with the help of the tsar's evil cousin. They burnt it and
gave the messenger another note instead:

The tsarina gave birth to a monster today.

When the tsar received this news, he was deeply sad-
dened. He sent the messenger home with this order:

Be silent about this matter and wait
until I return home and judge for myself.

But the envious sisters and the tsar's cousin once again
intercepted the messenger. They made him drunk with
wine, and stole the tsar's order, exchanging it for a letter
they had prepared. The letter read:

From Tsar Saltan to his knights:
Drown the tsarina and her child deep in the sea.

The knights wailed and wept when they heard about the tsar's order, but that night they went to the tsarina. They read her the false letter, then put her and the child into a large barrel. Fastening the lid, they sealed the cracks with tar and rolled the barrel into the sea.

The barrel floated on the waves for many days and nights. As storms raged, the waves rose and plunged. The stars crossed the heavens, the sun and moon rose and sank, and the tsar's son grew splendidly in the barrel.

But his mother wept and wailed so much that the child sang:

> *"Wave, oh wave, my friend so dear,*
> *take us to the land so near!"*

The wave heard this and washed the barrel ashore. But the tsarina still wailed, "We are imprisoned! How can we free ourselves from this barrel?"

Then the child sang once more:

> *"Barrel, my friend, do this for me,*
> *open yourself so we can be free!"*

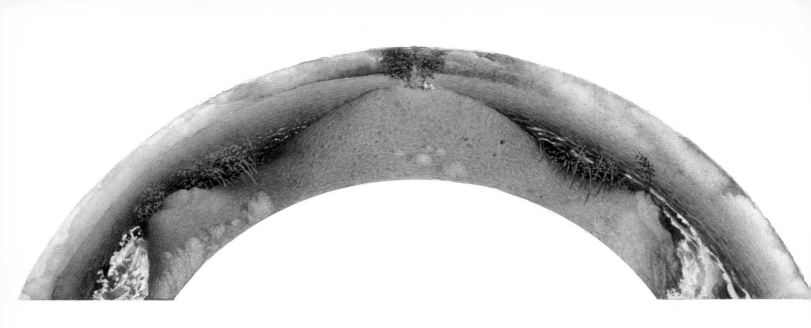

The barrel broke apart, and the tsarina and her son
climbed out. They saw that they had landed on a barren
island. By now the boy's stomach was rumbling with
hunger. He took some thick branches from an oak tree,
and along with a leather strap, he made himself a bow
and some arrows. As he looked around for something to
kill, he suddenly heard a wailing sound. In the ocean surf
he saw a swan, and over it a hawk was soaring.

He quickly put an arrow to the bowstring and hit the
hawk in the neck. The bird fell from the sky into the sea
with a loud scream, as though a human being had cried,
and the swan quickly killed it.

"Thank you, Tsarevitch!" the swan cried. "You have
freed me from a dark power. For I must tell you that I am
a princess, and the hawk was an evil and spiteful magi-
cian. Don't be sad that you have lost the bird! I will
always stay close to you and will fulfill all your wishes."
Then the swan disappeared and the tsarevitch, the young
prince, had to go to sleep that night as hungry as ever.

But when the boy and his mother awoke the next morning, they saw that a huge and splendid city had appeared. Where the deserted beach had been, a city with golden domes and towers, surrounded by a white wall, now took its place.

"Mother!" the tsarevitch called, "look what my swan has given us!" Hardly had they passed through the city gate when all the bells began to ring and gaily dressed people ran toward them. They called the tsarevitch their prince, placed a crown on his head, and led him to the palace.

From then on, the tsar's son ruled the land and was called Prince Guidon.

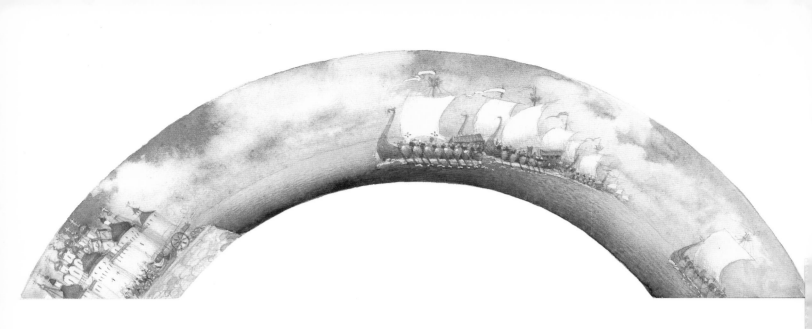

One day a strong wind came from the sea and a ship was blown onto the land. The sailors on the ship were very surprised to discover a new city with towers and battlements on what had been a bleak and barren island. They were greeted with ceremonial fireworks and were received by the people with great hospitality. The sailors told Prince Guidon that they were fur traders on their way to see the mighty Tsar Saltan. The prince asked them to give the tsar his kindest regards. He accompanied the merchants back to their ship and watched them leave. As he did so, there was a roar from the surf and the swan suddenly appeared.

"Why are you so sad, my prince?" the swan asked.

"Oh, I would like so much to see my father!" he answered longingly.

"Is that all you wish for?" the swan asked. "Follow the ship! Fly to your father—disguised as a gnat!"

And that is what happened. Changed into a gnat, the prince reached the trading ship and hid in a crack in the mast during the weeks of the journey.

When they finally reached land, he went with the fur traders to the tsar's palace. They were greeted with music and a wonderful meal. But Tsar Saltan, looking very depressed, sat between the cook and the weaver, with his cousin at his feet. He ordered the traders to tell him about their journey.

They told him about the amazing new city with its palaces and gardens that had appeared on the barren island. And they spoke of Prince Guidon on his golden throne and told the tsar that the prince sent his greetings.

"If I live long enough," the tsar said, "I'd like to see this city with my own eyes."

But the tsarina's sisters were still filled with mean envy, and the cook cried angrily, "It's not worth the journey! I know of a much more splendid miracle. In a forest far away there lives a squirrel in a fir tree, and this squirrel can sing and crack nuts. The nutshells are golden and the kernels are emeralds!"

Hearing this, the gnat flew to the cook's face and stung her on her eyelid. And before it began to swell, the gnat flew home over the blue sea and disappeared.

The next morning Prince Guidon walked along the beach. The swan appeared among the waves and asked the prince why he was so sad.

"Ah," said the prince, "I wish I had a squirrel like the one the cook described."

"Is that all?" the swan asked. "Go home, and you will find it."

And it was true. In the palace courtyard a fir tree had grown and a squirrel was sitting in its branches, singing and cracking golden nuts with emerald kernels!

One day the wind blew from the sea again and brought another ship on shore. These traders were also on their way to see Tsar Saltan, and Prince Guidon asked them to convey his greetings to the tsar. This time he followed them disguised as a fly.

When the traders reached the court of the tsar, they told him about the amazing city on the island, and the squirrel that cracked golden nuts. Hearing this, the tsar again said, "If I live long enough, I'd like to see this city!"

The sisters were filled with rage, and the weaver said, "It is not worth the journey. I know of a much more splendid miracle. Far away in the Northern Sea a bare beach rises, and like lightning, thirty-three knights in shining armor appear from the ocean."

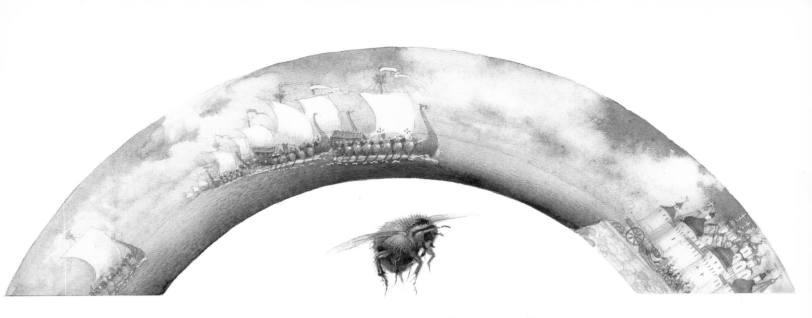

Upon hearing this, the fly was furious and stung the weaver in the eye, but before the weaver could cry out, the fly had disappeared beyond the blue sea.

The following day Prince Guidon told the swan what the weaver had said, and the swan granted his wish once again. Thirty-three knights appeared out of the raging sea, and offered to serve Prince Guidon.

A third time the wind blew a ship onto the island. The sailors saw the wonders of the city, the squirrel, and the thirty-three knights, and when they too went to see the tsar, they told him all about it. This time Prince Guidon had followed them disguised as a wasp.

Once again the tsar expressed a wish to be able to see all these miracles with his own eyes. And the three evil women were again seized with jealousy, and the tsar's cousin shouted, "It's not worth the journey! I know of a much more splendid miracle. A tsar's daughter lives far across the sea, and she is so beautiful that she makes the brightest day seem dim, and at night she glows like the sun. Her hair shines like moonlight and her forehead is a mass of stars."

As she said this, the wasp stung the cousin right in the middle of her nose and flew off.

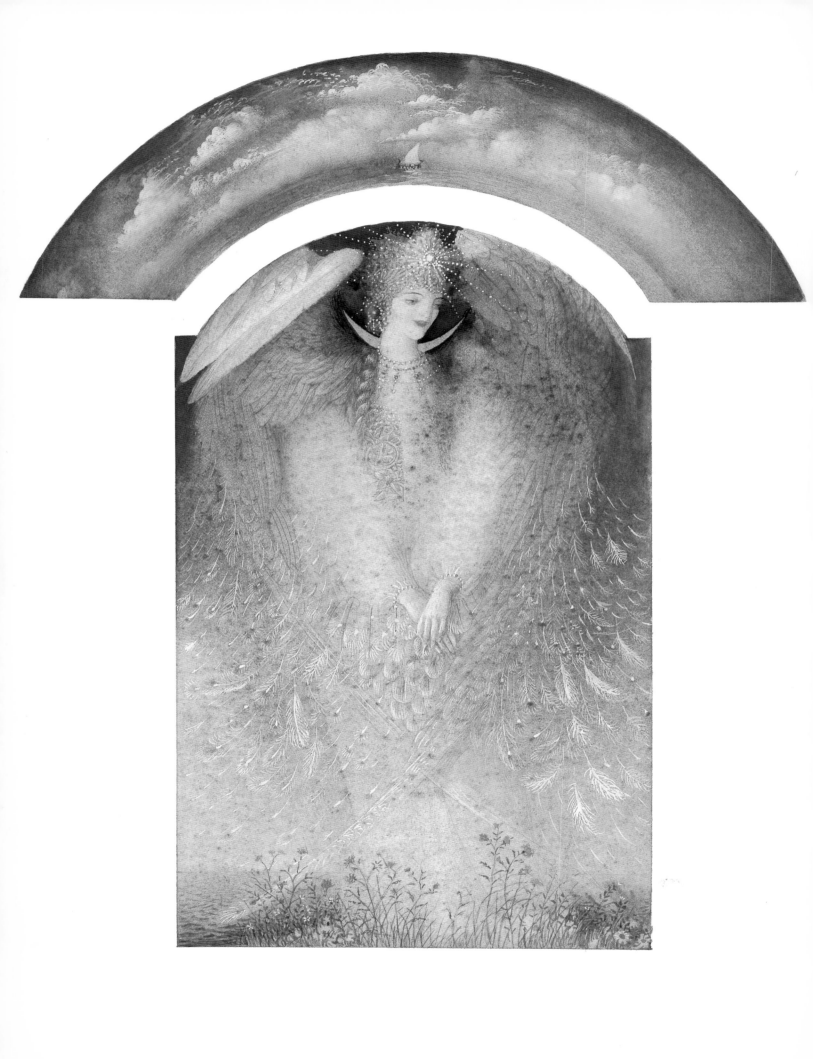

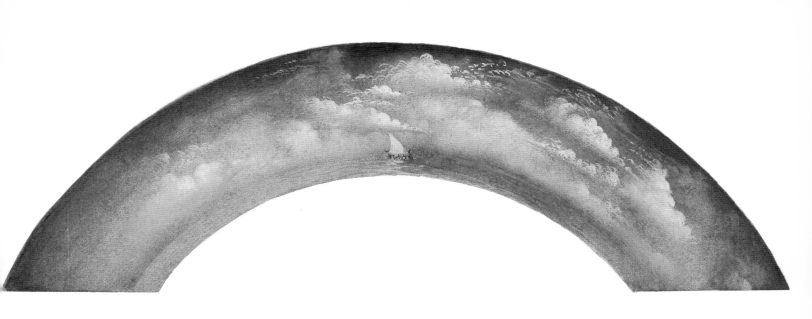

The next morning Prince Guidon walked sadly along the beach, and when the swan appeared and asked him why he was sad, he answered, "I would like to marry the tsar's daughter that the cousin was talking about, even if I had to go to the end of the world to find her!" Upon hearing this, the swan sighed and said, "There's no need for that! I am the tsar's daughter!" Her feathers fell from her and she was more beautiful than words could describe. The tsarina was delighted to give her son and the swan maiden her blessing. But hardly had the two of them been married when the wind blew another ship on land.

The merchants saw the miracles of the city, the squirrel, the thirty-three knights, and the swan maiden, and they set off to tell Tsar Saltan about it. This time the prince stayed at home.

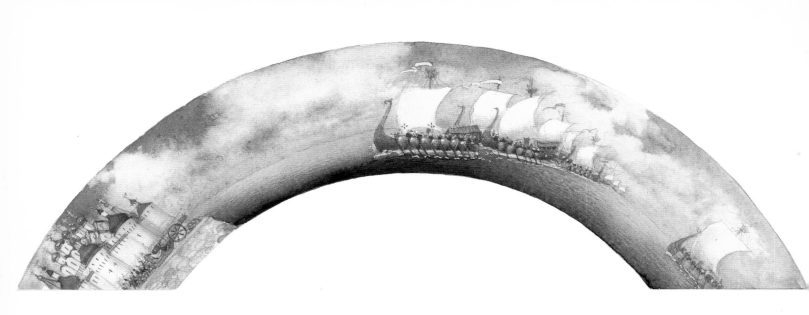

Tsar Saltan was no longer willing to be kept at home by the three wicked women. He sailed across the sea with a large fleet and reached the city on the island, and was welcomed with great honors. The prince came to greet him, and the tsar recognized his beloved wife standing next to the prince. Then he knew that Prince Guidon was the son he had long believed to be dead, and he embraced him, full of joy.

And because he was so happy, he forgave the two sisters and his cousin, but he forbade them ever to come to the amazing island of the swan maiden.

The tsar remained there, however, and they all celebrated a feast that lasted for days and weeks. And they all lived happily ever after.

DATE		